KV-193-577

THE WOODEN HORSE

PANDORA'S BOX

DONATED BY

ASSOCIATION OF PARENTS AND FRIENDS
OF
FARNBOROUGH PRIMARY SCHOOL

LONDON BOROUGH OF
FARNBOROUGH
PRIMARY SCHOOL
BROMLEY

For Mrs Clarke

THE WOODEN HORSE

PANDORA'S BOX

GERALDINE McCAUGHREAN
ILLUSTRATED BY TONY ROSS

ORCHARD BOOKS

ORCHARD BOOKS
96 Leonard Street, London EC2A 4RH
Orchard Books Australia
14 Mars Road, Lane Cove, NSW 2066
ISBN 1 86039 440 X (hardback)
ISBN 1 86039 533 3 (paperback)
First published in Great Britain 1997
Text © Geraldine McCaughrean 1992
Illustrations © Tony Ross 1997
1 2 3 4 5 6 02 01 00 99 98 97
The right of Geraldine McCaughrean to be identified as the
author and Tony Ross as the illustrator of this
work has been asserted by them in accordance with the
Copyright, Designs and Patents Act, 1988.
A CIP catalogue record for this book is available from the
British Library.
Printed in Great Britain

THE WOODEN HORSE

There was once a woman who hatched from an egg, like a bird. But she was more beautiful than any bird who ever flew. She was called Helen and there was not a prince, nor a duke, nor a king who did not want to win her. But she married old King Menelaus and lived in a palace on the shores of his kingdom.

If only that had put an end to the hopes of all the other princes, dukes and kings!

Young, handsome
Paris, Prince of Troy,
found Helen too
beautiful to forget,
and wanted too much
to have her for his
own. So he stole
Helen's love and ran
away with her to
Troy—the city called
the City of Horses.

King Menelaus grieved—but his grief then turned to anger—and, calling together an army of fifty thousand men, he sailed for Troy to get back his wife. He took with him the greatest heroes of the world: Achilles the brave, Odysseus the cunning, and Ajax the proud. A thousand ships put ashore outside the tall white walls of Troy.

Helen looked
out of her palace
window and
saw the fleet
approaching.
"What will
happen now?"
she wondered. "Who will win me?
Which side do I want to win?"

For weeks, for months, for years the Greeks lay siege to the city. The great heroes of Troy fought in single combat with the great heroes of Greece, sword against sword, chariot against chariot. But it decided nothing.

After ten years, Achilles the brave was dead. Ajax the proud lay in a grave covered with flowers. And Paris was dead and his lips too cold for kissing. So many good men had been killed. And those who had lived were sadder, wearier, older. Only Helen remained as lovely as ever—a precious prize locked inside Troy.

At last Odysseus
the cunning spoke up.
"I think I know how
we can get inside
the city of Troy."
The Greeks
listened eagerly.

"It'll never work!" said some.

"It's too dangerous!" said others.

But old King
Menelaus
nodded and
said, "Do it,
Odysseus."

For days the
Trojans, inside their walls, could hear
nothing but sawing and hammering.

Then one morning they looked over their high walls and saw ... a horse. A huge wooden horse.

They also saw that the Greeks had packed up their tents, launched their ships and set sail.

"They've gone! They've gone!" cheered the Trojans. "We've won the war! ... But what's this they've left behind? A horse?" They crept outside to look.

"It's a tribute to Troy!" said some. "A tribute to the City of Horses!"

"It's a trick," said others.

One man threw a spear at the wooden horse and it struck with a hollow thud. "Beware of Greeks even when they give you presents!" he warned.

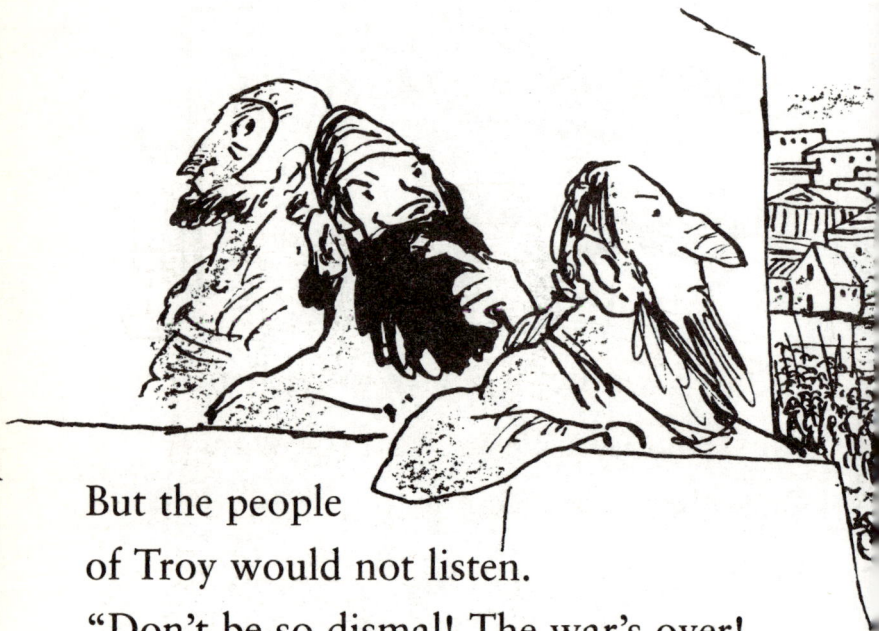

But the people
of Troy would not listen.
"Don't be so dismal! The war's over!
The Greeks have gone, haven't they?"

They began to celebrate, to drink wine and to dance. And they towed the huge wooden horse, on long ropes, in through the gates of Troy.

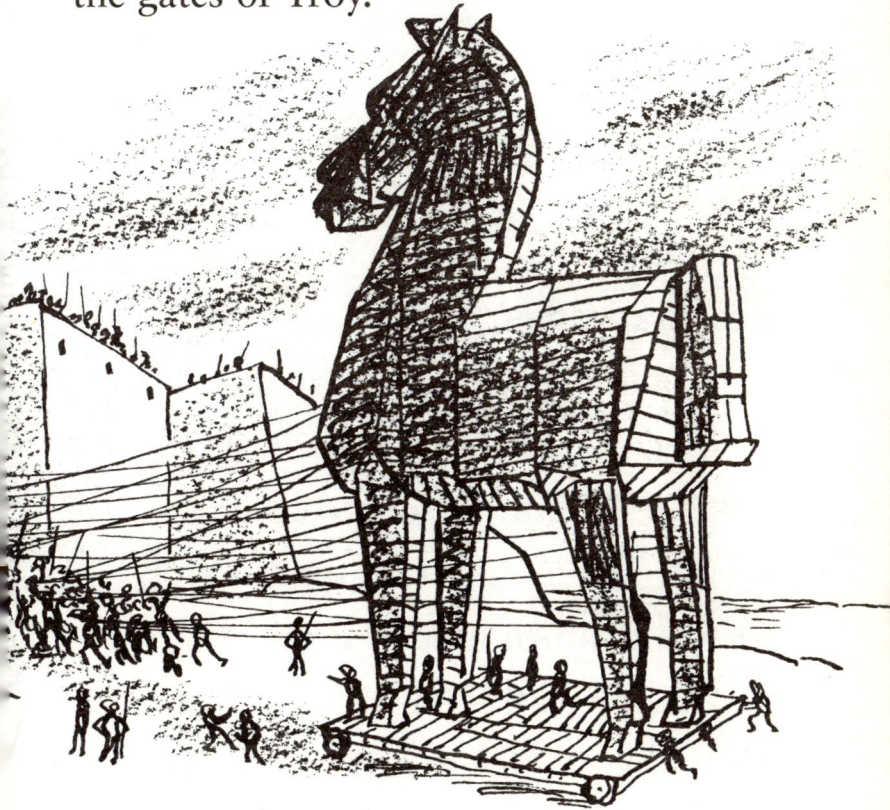

Meanwhile, inside the horse's hollow body, a dozen Greek soldiers crouched as still as stones. There was so little room in their hiding place that they were all pressed together, knee against knee, elbow against ear.

"Heave!" cried the Trojans, as they pulled the giant horse into the city square. The bumpy ride fogged and bruised the men hidden inside, but they held their breath and gripped their swords tight. One sneeze and they would be found out!

Helen looked out of
her window and saw
the horse, all decorated
now with flowers and
ribbons. She was a
Greek and knew the
ways of the Greeks
and she thought to
herself, "This is a trick." She turned
away from the window, put a finger to
her lips and sat quite still waiting.

The happy Trojans danced all day round the long legs of the wooden horse. At last, weary with joy, they tottered home to sleep, and the city fell silent.

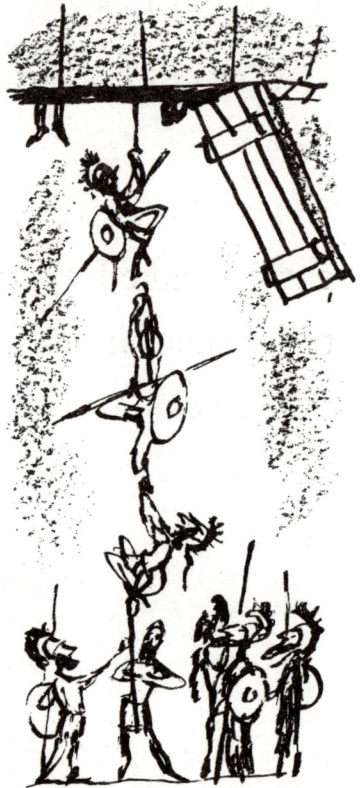

Then a secret door creaked open in the stomach of the horse. Down dropped a knotted rope. Down the rope climbed the dozen Greeks.

Meanwhile, the whole Greek fleet of ships sailed back to shore: they had only been hiding over the sea's horizon, waiting. As they pelted up the beach, they peered through the early morning darkness at the high, heavy city gates, anxious to see whether their plan had succeeded.

And there! The gates creaked open to let them in and the Greeks dashed through, swords at the ready.

A war that had lasted ten years was over. They set light to Troy's tall buildings. They killed Troy's young men. Then they seized Helen and sailed away. By morning there was nothing but the sound of weeping within Troy's charred and crumbling walls.

And Helen lived once more in the palace of King Menelaus on the shores of his kingdom. If she had loved Paris once, she never said so, and never spoke his name, and she and Menelaus lived happily ever after.

PANDORA'S BOX

LONDON BOROUGH OF
FARNBOROUGH
PRIMARY SCHOOL
BROMLEY

At the very beginning, the gods ruled
over an empty world. From their home
on Mount Olympus, where they lived
in halls of sunlight and cloud, they
looked out over oceans and islands,
woodland and hill. But nothing moved
in the landscape because there were no
animals or birds or people.

Zeus, king of the gods, gave
Prometheus and his brother Epimetheus
the task of making living creatures, and
he sent them down to live on earth.

Epimetheus made turtles and gave them shells; he made horses and gave them tails and manes. He made anteaters and gave them long noses and longer tongues; he made birds and gave them the gift of flight. But although Epimetheus was a wonderful craftsman, he was not nearly as clever as his brother.

So Prometheus watched over his
brother's work and, when all the
animals and birds, insects and fishes
were made, it was Prometheus who
made the very last creature of all. He
took soil and mixed it into mud, and
out of that he moulded First Man.

"I'll make him just like us gods—
two legs, two arms and upright—not
crawling on all fours. All the other
beasts spend their days looking at the
ground, but Man will look at the stars!"

When he had finished, Prometheus
was very proud of what he had made.
But when it came to giving Man a gift,
there was nothing left to give!

"Give him a tail," said Epimetheus. But all the tails had gone. "Give him a trunk," Epimetheus suggested. But the elephant already had that. "Give him fur," said Epimetheus, but all the fur had been used up.

Suddenly Prometheus exclaimed, "I know what to give him!" He climbed up to heaven—up as high as the fiery chariot of the sun. And from the rim of its bright wheel he stole one tiny sliver of fire. It was such a very small flame that he was able to hide it inside a stalk of grass and hurry back to the earth without any of the gods seeing what he was up to.

But the secret could not be kept for long. Next time Zeus looked down from Mount Olympus, he saw something glimmering red and yellow under a column of grey smoke. "Prometheus, what have you done? You've given the secret of fire to those ... those ... mud-men! Bad enough that you make them look like gods, now you go sharing our belongings with them! So! You put your little mud-people before us, do you? I'll make you sorry you ever made them! I'll make you sorry you were ever made yourself!"

And he tied Prometheus to a cliff and sent eagles to peck at him all day long. You or I would have died. But the gods can never die. Prometheus knew that the pain would never end, that the eagles would never stop and that his chains would never break. A terrible hopelessness tore at his heart and hurt him more than the eagles could ever do.

Zeus was just as angry with Man for accepting the gift of fire, but you would never have thought so. He was busy making him another wonderful present.

With the help of the other gods, he shaped First Woman. Venus gave her beauty, Mercury gave her a clever tongue, Apollo taught her how to play sweet music. Finally Zeus draped a veil over her lovely head and named her Pandora.

Then, with a grin on his face, he sent for Epimetheus (who was not quite clever enough to suspect a trick).

"Here's a bride for you, Epimetheus —a reward for all your hard work making the animals. And here's a wedding present for you both. But whatever you do, don't open it."

The wedding present was a wooden chest, bolted and padlocked and bound with a band of iron. When he reached his home at the foot of Mount Olympus, Epimetheus set the chest down in a dark corner, covered it with a blanket, and put it out of his mind. After all, with Pandora for a bride, what more could a man possibly want?

In those days the world was a wonderful place to live. No one was sad. Nobody ever grew old or ill. And Epimetheus married Pandora; she came to live in his house, and everything she wanted he gave her.

But sometimes, when she caught sight of the chest, Pandora would say, "What a strange wedding present. Why can't we open it?"

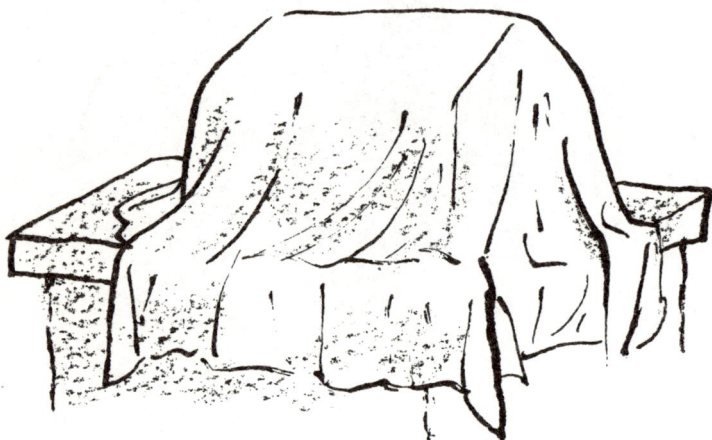

"Never mind why. Remember, you must never touch it," Epimetheus would reply sharply. "Not touch at all. Do you hear?"

"Of course I won't touch it. It's only an old chest. What do I want with an old chest? ... What do you think is inside?"

"Never mind what's inside. Put it out of your mind."

And Pandora did try. She really did. But one day, when Epimetheus was out, she just could not forget about the chest and somehow she found herself standing right beside it.

"No!" she told herself. "I expect it's full of cloth—or dishes—or papers. Something dull." She bustled about the house. She tried to read. Then...

"Let us out!"

"Who said that?"

"Do let us out, Pandora!"

Pandora looked out of the window.
But in her heart of hearts she knew that
the voice was coming from the chest.
She pulled back the blanket with finger
and thumb. The voice was louder now:
"Please, please do let us out, Pandora!"

"I can't. I mustn't." She crouched
down beside the chest.

"Oh, but you have to. We want you
to. We need you to, Pandora!"

"But I promised!" Her fingers
stroked the latch.

"It's easy. The key's in
the lock," said the little
voice—a purring little voice.

It was. A big golden key.

"No. No, I mustn't," she told herself.

"But you do want to, Pandora. And why shouldn't you? It was your wedding present too, wasn't it? ... Oh, all right, don't let us out. Just peep inside. What harm can that do?"

Pandora's heart beat faster.

Click. The key turned.

Clack. Clack. The latches were unlatched.

BANG!

The lid flew back and Pandora was
knocked over by an icy wind full of grit.
It filled the room with howling. It tore
the curtains and stained them brown.
And after the wind came slimy things,
growling snarling things, claws and
snouts, revolting things too nasty to
look at, all slithering out of the chest.

"I'm Disease," said one.

"I'm Cruelty," said another.

"I'm Pain, and she's Old Age."

"I'm Disappointment and he's Hate."

"I'm Jealousy and that one there is War."

"AND I AM DEATH!" said the smallest purring voice.

The creatures leapt and scuttled and oozed out through the windows, and at once all the flowers shrivelled, and the fruit on the trees grew mouldy. The sky itself turned a filthy yellow, and the sound of crying filled the town.

Mustering all her strength, Pandora slammed down the lid of the chest. But there was one creature left inside.

"No, no, Pandora! If you shut me inside, that will be your worst mistake of all! Let me go!"

"Oh no! you don't fool me twice," sobbed Pandora.

"But I am Hope!" whispered the little voice faintly. "Without me the world won't be able to bear all the unhappiness you have turned loose!"

So Pandora lifted the lid, and a white flicker, small as a butterfly, flitted out and was blown this way and that by the howling winds. And as it fluttered through the open window, a watery sun came out and shone on the wilted garden.

Chained to his cliff, Prometheus could
do nothing to help the
little mud-people he
had made. Though
he writhed and
strained, there was
no breaking free. All
around him he could
hear the sound of crying. Now that the
snarling creatures had been let loose,
there would be no more easy days or
peaceful nights for men and women!
They would be unkind, afraid, greedy,
unhappy. And one day they must all die
and go to live as ghosts in the cold
dark Underworld. The thought of it
almost broke Prometheus' heart.

Then, out of the corner of his eye, he glimpsed a little white flicker of light and felt something, small as a butterfly, touch his bare breast. Hope came to rest over his heart.

He felt a sudden strength, a sort of courage. He was sure that his life was not over. "No matter how bad things are today, tomorrow may be better," he thought. "One day someone may come this way—take pity on me—break these chains and set me free. One day!"

The eagles pecked at the fluttering shred of light but were too slow to catch it in their beaks. Hope fluttered on its way, blowing round the world like a single tiny tongue of flame.

LONDON
FARNBOROUGH
PRIMARY SCHOOL
BROMLEY